Created by
Jim Davis

Written by Mark Acey
Designed and Illustrated by Mike Fentz

PAWS, INC.

Watermill Press

Copyright © 1994 United Feature Syndicate, Inc. All rights reserved. Published by Watermill Press, an imprint of Troll Associates, Inc. No part of this book may be reproduced or utilized in any form or by any means, electronic or mechanical, including photocopying, recording, or by any information storage or retrieval system, without written permission from the publisher.
Printed in the United States of America.
10 9 8 7 6 5 4 3 2 1

"Hey, Garfield, listen to this," said Jon as he was reading the newspaper. "It says here a woman was cleaning out her attic and discovered a chest full of treasure worth a million dollars!"

Garfield's ears immediately perked up.

"Wow! That sure would buy a lot of donuts!" said Garfield.

"Who knows? There might even be treasure in *our* attic," joked Jon. "No one's been up there in ages — except maybe some spiders."

Garfield cringed at the mere thought of those creepy creatures.

"I'll tell you what," said Jon. "If you and Odie will clean out the attic while I'm visiting Aunt Lola, you can keep whatever treasure you find. And if you don't find anything, well, at least we'll have a nice clean room."

"Don't hold your breath," cracked Garfield. "The only thing I intend to clean out is the refrigerator."

But after Jon left, Garfield found himself thinking more and more about hidden treasure. His curiosity soon triumphed over his laziness and fear of spiders, and in no time Garfield and his dust-busting buddy, Odie, were in the attic.

"Look at this mess!" exclaimed Garfield, as they gazed in horror at the dusty, junk-filled room. "We don't need a broom — we need a bulldozer! Let's get out of here! No treasure is worth this much work!"

But then, as fate would have it, Odie unleashed an enormous sneeze that sent dust — and Garfield — flying. Like a furry missile, Garfield hurtled across the room and smacked headlong into an old picture of a clown hanging above a boarded-up fireplace. And that's when it happened . . .

Suddenly, the entire fireplace swiveled halfway around, revealing a small open space.

"A secret compartment!" gasped Garfield, still dazed and wobbly. "I must have triggered some hidden mechanism when I hit that picture. And look, Odie, there's a trunk inside! This is it! I'm rich!"

"Grrrr," growled Odie.

"Okay, so *we're* rich," added Garfield hastily. "I guess your contribution was nothing to sneeze at. Anyway, don't just stand there . . . help me get this thing open."

The two treasure-hunters quickly hauled out the trunk and flung it open. Like a jack-in-the-box, out sprang a strange little ghost. Haunting laughter filled the air.

"Great Caesar's ghost!" screamed Garfield.

"Close, but no cigar," replied the ghost. "Actually, Hugo P. Roisterdoister's my name and comedy's my game! And that's no joke! HA! HA! HA! HA! HA!!!!!"

"Knock, knock," said the ghost.
"Huh?" mumbled Garfield, who was very confused.
"Knock, knock," repeated the ghost.
"Uh, who's there?" answered Garfield.
"Boo," said the ghost.
"Boo who?" replied Garfield.
"Don't cry . . . I'm a *friendly* ghost! HAAAA! Get it? Boo hoo! Don't cry. YUK! YUK! YUK!"

Garfield and Odie just rolled their eyes and shrugged.

"Let me get this straight," said Garfield. "You're a ghost?"

"Last time I checked," said the ghost.

"And your name is Hugo P. Roosterdooster?" continued Garfield.

"Roisterdoister. Hugo P. Roisterdoister. That's my name . . . don't wear it out! But you can call me Hugo. Or you can call me Wacko. Or you can —"

"Okay, we get the idea," interrupted Garfield.

But there was no stopping Hugo.

"Don't stop me . . . I'm on a roll! I'm the ghost with the most! Hey, did you hear the one about the chicken who got sick? He had people pox! SNORT! Speaking of chickens . . . know what side a rooster has the most feathers on? The *out*side! WAHOOOO! Don't applaud . . . just throw money!"

All afternoon Hugo tortured Garfield and Odie with his corny jokes.

"I can't take it anymore," groaned Garfield, covering his ears. "Let's make a break for it, Odie."

But Hugo was hot on their trail.

"What's the matter, boy? Got sensitive ears? I knew a guy with sensitive ears. He yelled every time I yanked them! HARDYHARHAR!"

Garfield and Odie zoomed from room to room. On and on they ran, and on and on AND ON went Hugo's awful jokes, each one followed by a nutty chuckle, giggle, or guffaw. Finally Garfield and Odie ducked into a closet and closed the door.

"Listen," whispered Garfield. "I think we've lost him. At last, a little peace and quiet."

But no sooner had Garfield uttered those words than Hugo materialized right through the door!

"TAH-DAH! But seriously folks . . . what do you get when you cross a dog with an elephant? A squashed dog!"

A loud laugh echoed through the closet. But this time it was not Hugo snickering and snorting — it was Garfield!

"Now that's more like it," said Hugo, finally calming down. "I was wondering what a ghost had to do to get a laugh around here."

"Try telling funnier jokes — like that one about the squashed dog," said Garfield. "You've got to admit that your material is a little on the stale side."

"Hey, your jokes would be old, too, if you had been cooped up in that trunk for the last fifty years."

"What were you doing in there, anyway?" asked Garfield as they left the closet.

"Not much," replied Hugo. "That trunk didn't have a lot of leg room — not that I have any legs! HAAAA! But seriously . . . I once haunted theaters and dance halls before 'The Amusing Arbuckle' —"

"Hey, that was Jon's grandfather, the old comedian!" said Garfield.

"Don't interrupt, son. I've got half a century of lost time to make up for. Like I was saying, I used to have a life before I got trapped in that loony Arbuckle's trick trunk and stuffed behind the fireplace. What a weird guy he was!"

"It must run in the family," thought Garfield.

"Ever since then," continued Hugo, "I've been telling the same jokes to myself over and over. Fortunately, I've never told a joke I didn't like. YUK! YUK! All joking aside, it's been really lonely. You're not going to make me go back in there, are you?"

"Well, uh," hesitated Garfield. "I really don't think Jon wants a ghost in the house."

Tears began spouting from Hugo's eyes.

"For crying out loud," sighed Garfield. "I hate to see a grown ghost cry."

"I'll do anything," pleaded Hugo. "Birthday parties . . . séances . . . Halloween bashes. Just give me an audience!"

"What am I supposed to do?" asked Garfield, throwing up his paws. "All the old theaters and dance halls closed down years ago. I'm afraid you'll just — HEY! That gives me an idea! It's a long-shot, but it's the only shot we've got. Follow me. We're going on a little trip."

Garfield led Hugo and Odie to an old abandoned building.

"It's my old haunt!" whooped Hugo. "The Tons of Fun Theatre. My ghost pals and I were *frightfully* happy here. TEE HEE! How did you know?"

"I didn't," said Garfield. "But the legend around town is that this building is haunted. That's why it's never been torn down—people are too afraid to come near it."

"My friends must still be here then," said Hugo excitedly. "Well, I hate to joke and run, but it's time to scare up some fun! HOO HOO! I'm a poet and I don't even know it! YUK! YUK! I've got a million of 'em. Come on, let's get this show on the road . . ."

Hugo zipped through the door of the theater.

"Hey, wait for us!" yelled Garfield.

Garfield yanked open the door.

"Uh, you first, Odie."

"Good evening, ladies and germs!" said Hugo.

"Hugo?" squealed a ghost. "Hugo P. Roisterdoister?"

"That's my name. Ask me again and I'll tell you the same," said Hugo.

Instantly, the building erupted into a chorus of ghostly laughter.

"Let's hear it for my furry friends who helped me get back here," cried Hugo.

Whistling and clapping echoed throughout the theater.

"Don't applaud . . . just throw money!" quipped Garfield.

"HAAAA! Now you're getting into the *spirit*!" roared Hugo. "Hey, why don't you stick around?"

"No, thanks. We've caught your act already," said Garfield. "Maybe we'll see you later."

"Not if I see you first!" snorted Hugo, waving goodbye.

Garfield and Odie left the old theater, which was ringing with ghostly guffaws.

"Well, Odie," said Garfield. "I'm glad Hugo's finally back where he belongs. You know what they say, 'Be it ever so haunted, there's no place like home!'"